D0960920

Disney

# Winnie the Pooh

# Forever Friends

By Lisa Ann Marsoli

Illustrated by Disney Storybook Artists

Disney PRESS

NEW YORK

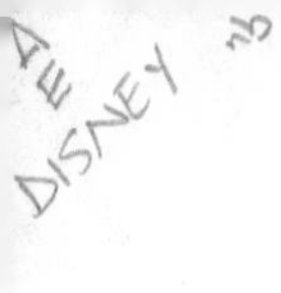

For information, address Disney Press, 114 Fifth Avenue, New York, New York 10011-5690.

Based on the "Winnie the Pooh" works by A.A. Milne and E.H. Shepard

First Edition
Library of Congress Cataloging-in-Publication Data on file.
ISBN 978-1-4231-3578-4

J689-1817-1-11046

Manufactured in the USA
For more Disney Press fun, visit www.disneybooks.com

goes to visit .

Pooh Christopher Robin

There is a on the door.

note

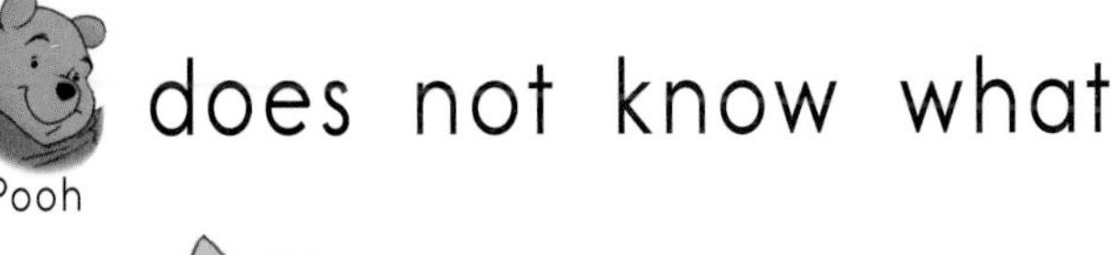

does not know what

Pooh

the says.

note

Owl looks at the note.

"'Gone out. Backson,'" reads Owl.

"Oh, dear! A Backson has !"
Christopher Robin

 is scared.
Owl

"What is a Backson?" asks 

.

says that a Backson is a monster!

He draws a picture of it.

Now [Piglet] is scared.

"What does a  do?"


asks  .

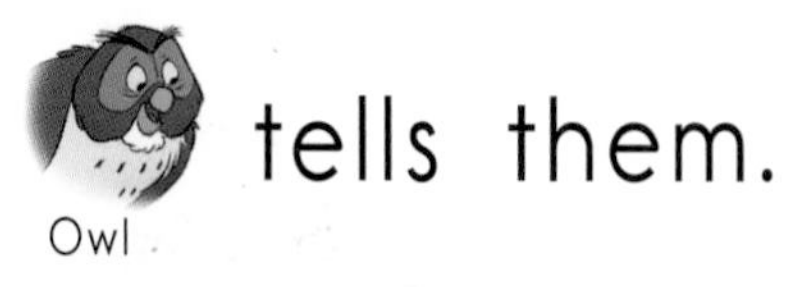 tells them.

A  stops clocks.

Backson

A  puts holes in socks.

Backson

A  scribbles in books.

Backson

A  sounds mean!

Backson

Now *everyone* is scared!

But Rabbit has a plan.

They will lead the [Backson] into a trap.

Then they will save [Christopher Robin]!

Some of the friends go get things to make a trail.

They will collect them in a wagon.

Pooh and Piglet head off to set the trap.

They need a cloth, a shovel, and a honeypot.

digs a pit with his .
Piglet shovel

"Good job!" says .
Pooh

They cover the pit with a cloth.

They use the shovel to add

a pot of honey.

It is a Backson trap!

*Hip-hip-hooray! Friends will save the day!*

Now all the friends take

things from the wagon.

They leave a trail in the

Hundred-Acre Wood.

They go back to the pit.

Everyone falls in but Piglet.

They do not trap the Backson.

They trap themselves!

Piglet
wants to get his friends out.

He tries to use what is left in the 
wagon
.

It does not work.

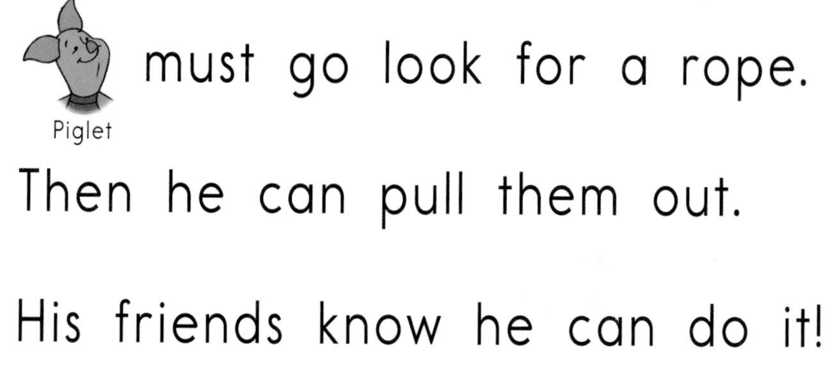 Piglet must go look for a rope.

Then he can pull them out.

His friends know he can do it!

*Hip-hip-hooray!*  Piglet *will save the day!*

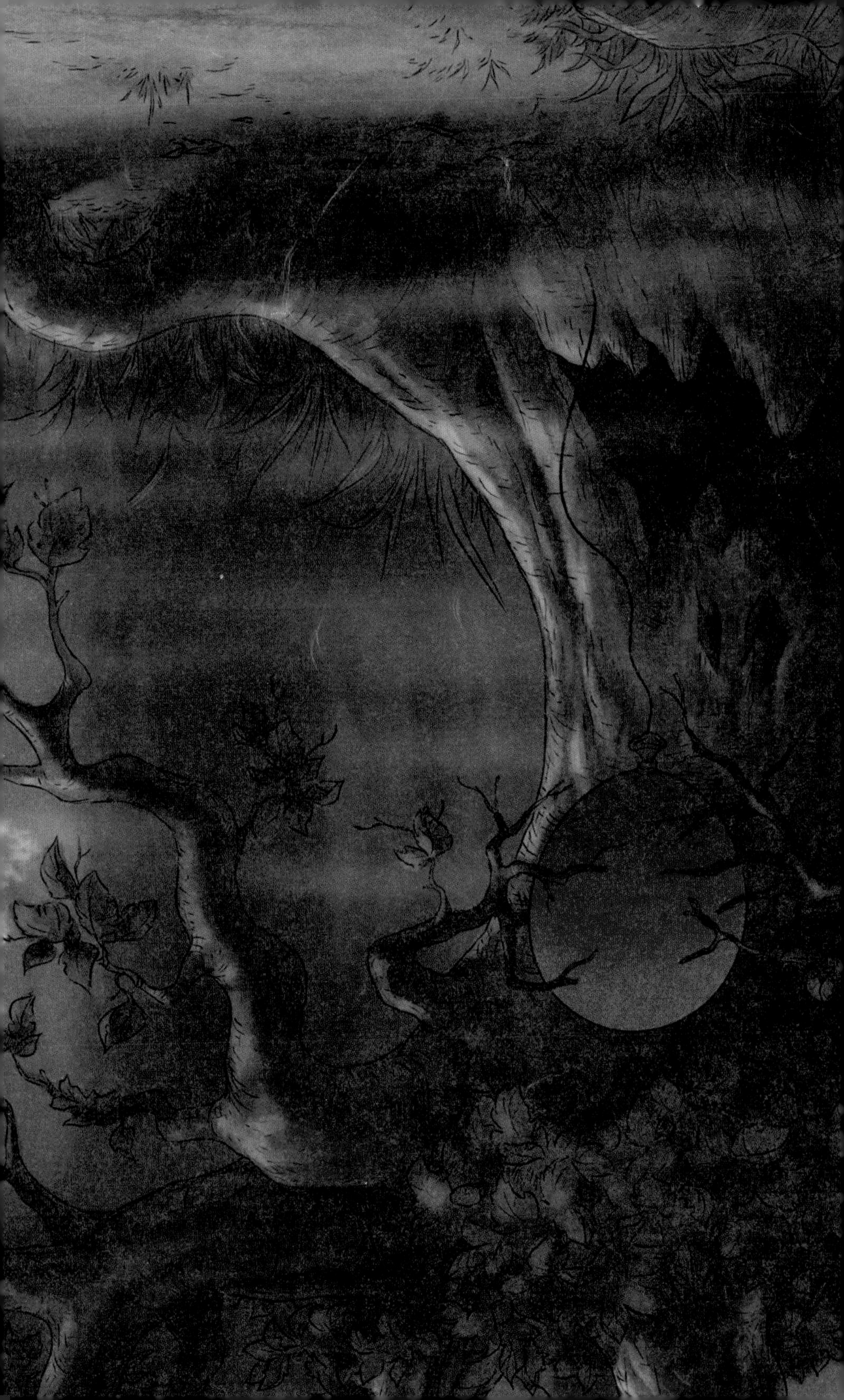

Piglet walks along.
He thinks he sees a monster!
Piglet runs away.

It is just B'loon stuck in a tree.

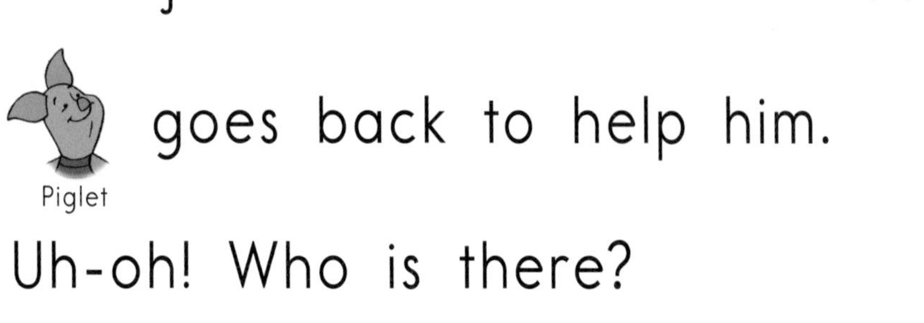


goes back to help him.

Uh-oh! Who is there?

"Backson!" cries Piglet.

He saves B'loon and runs away.

*Hip-hip-hooray! Piglet will save the day!*

falls into the pit.

It is B'loon's turn to help.

*Hip-hip-hooray! B'loon*
*will save the day!*

B'loon will take [Christopher Robin] to his friends.

Soon everyone is out of

the pit.

They ask about the Backson.

"What Backson?" Christopher Robin asks.

His note says "back soon"—not

Backson!

Now Pooh sees that Eeyore needs help.

His tail is missing.

Everyone looks for it.

*Hip-hip-hooray! Friends will save the day!*

 finds the tail.
Pooh

It is hanging from Owl's doorbell!

"I thought no one wanted it,"

says  .
Owl

Pooh brings the tail to Christopher Robin.

Christopher Robin puts it back where it should be.

"Everyone did a good job of helping each other today," says 

.

"That's what friends do," 

replies.

*Hip-hip-hooray! Friends DID save the day!*